BIG BOB AND THE THANKSGIVING POTATOES

by Daniel Pinkwater
Illustrated by Jill Pinkwater

Hello Reader! — Level 3

SCHOLASTIC INC. Cartwheel BOOKS®

New York Toronto London Auckland Sydney

Big Bob

My name is Bob. I am big. Big Bob. That's what they call me. I weigh 79 pounds. I am 55 inches tall.

Most kids in second grade weigh about 54 pounds. They are about 49 inches tall. I am bigger. Big Bob.

There are problems with being big. You stand out. You look like you don't belong. The kids laugh at you. You feel clumsy. You feel dumb.

Hello, Family Members,

Learning to read is one of the most important accomplishments of early childhood. **Hello Reader!** books are designed to help children become skilled readers who like to read. Beginning readers learn to read by remembering frequently used words like "the," "is," and "and"; by using phonics skills to decode new words; and by interpreting picture and text clues. These books provide both the stories children enjoy and the structure they need to read fluently and independently. Here are suggestions for helping your child *before*, *during*, and *after* reading:

Before

- Look at the cover and pictures and have your child predict what the story is about.
- Read the story to your child.
- Encourage your child to chime in with familiar words and phrases.
- Echo read with your child by reading a line first and having your child read it after you do.

During

- Have your child think about a word he or she does not recognize right away. Provide hints such as "Let's see if we know the sounds" and "Have we read other words like this one?"
- Encourage your child to use phonics skills to sound out new words.
- Provide the word for your child when more assistance is needed so that he or she does not struggle and the experience of reading with you is a positive one.
- Encourage your child to have fun by reading with a lot of expression . . . like an actor!

After

- Have your child keep lists of interesting and favorite words.
- Encourage your child to read the books over and over again. Have him or her read to brothers, sisters, grandparents, and even teddy bears. Repeated readings develop confidence in young readers.
- Talk about the stories. Ask and answer questions. Share ideas about the funniest and most interesting characters and events in the stories.

I do hope that you and your child enjoy this book.

— Francie Alexander
Reading Specialist,
Scholastic's Instructional Publishing Group

To Marilyn Wann

Text copyright © 1998 by Daniel Pinkwater.
Illustrations copyright © 1998 by Jill Pinkwater.
All rights reserved. Published by Scholastic Inc.
SCHOLASTIC, HELLO READER! and CARTWHEEL BOOKS and associated logos are trademarks and/or registered trademarks of Scholastic Inc.

Library of Congress Cataloging-in-Publication Data

Pinkwater, Daniel Manus.
    Big Bob and the Thanksgiving potatoes / by Daniel Pinkwater; illustrated by Jill Pinkwater.
        p.   cm.—(Hello reader! Level 3)
    "Cartwheel Books."
    Summary: Big Bob and Big Gloria, who are friends because they are both large for their age, start a new trend when their second-grade class is supposed to make turkey decorations for Thanksgiving.
    ISBN 0-590-64095-X
    [1. Thanksgiving Day—Fiction.   2. Schools—Fiction.   3. Size—Fiction.]   I. Pinkwater, Jill, ill.   II. Title.   III. Series.
PZ7.P6335Bg   1998
[E]—dc21   98-6595
                                                                              CIP
                                                                              AC
12 11 10 9 8 7 6 5   02 03

                        Printed in the U.S.A.   24
            First printing, November 1998

I would not have minded being a little bigger. But I am a lot bigger. Big Bob.

When you are big, you always sit in the back of the room. When you do something wrong or make a mistake, the teacher says, "Bob, I am surprised at you. A big boy like you should know better."

Being big is no day at the beach.

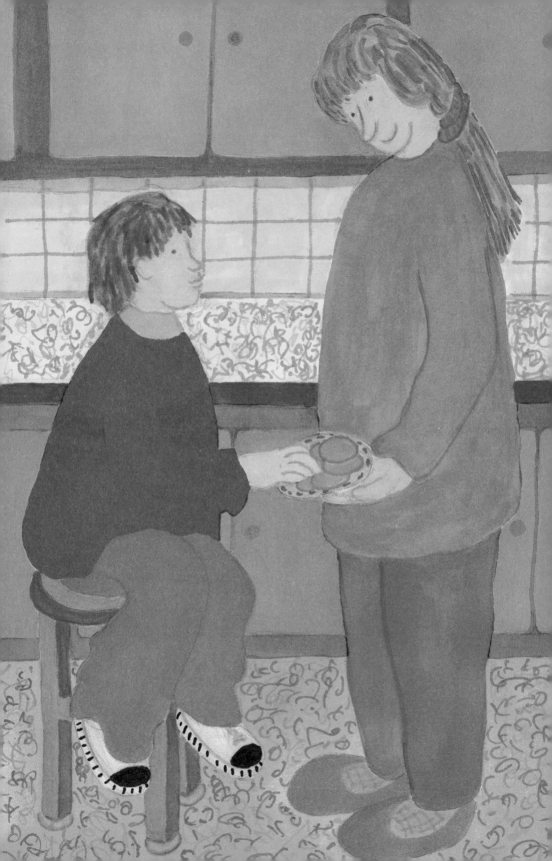

I told my mother, "The kids don't like me because I am big."

"Oh, I am sure that they like you," my mother said.

"They don't," I told my mother. "They laugh at me. They think I am clumsy. They think I am dumb."

I started to cry.

"Now, don't cry," my mother said. "You shouldn't cry. You're a big boy."

Everybody in my family is big. I don't feel that I am the wrong size when I am with my family. I feel just right when I am with my family. I feel just wrong when I am at school.

I am as big as a fifth grader, but the fifth graders want nothing to do with me because I am only a second grader. When I play in the playground with second graders, I often squash them. I don't mean to, of course.

People may not want you for a friend when you squash them.

Life can be difficult when you are big.

Big Boris

I have a dog. Boris. Boris is big like
me. We go swimming. We go for walks.
Boris lets me use him as a pillow when I
read. Sometimes I read stories to Boris.
Boris is my friend.

Big Gloria

I have another friend. It is Gloria. Gloria is in the second grade, too. Gloria is big. She is bigger than I am. We became friends because we are big, but we stay friends because we like each other.

Billy Thimble is a boy in second grade. "Your best friend is a girl," Billy Thimble said.

"So?" I asked Billy Thimble.

Tina Tiny is a girl in second grade. "You are a boy. Your best friend should be a boy," Tina Tiny said.

"Why?" I asked Tina Tiny.

"Boys should have boys as best friends, and girls should have girls as best friends," Tina Tiny said.

"You are weird," Billy Thimble said.

"And you are silly," Big Gloria said. "We are friends, and that is that."

"You are friends and you are too big," Billy Thimble and Tina Tiny said.

"We are big," Big Gloria said. "Now go away."

"Go away?"

"Go away or behave nicely," Big Gloria said.

"Behave nicely?"

"Behave nicely or we will squash you," Big Gloria said.

"Oh, no! Don't squash us," Billy Thimble and Tina Tiny said. "We will behave nicely."

"Good," Big Gloria said. "Here is a banana."

"Good one, Gloria," I said.

"I know," Big Gloria said.

Mr. Salami

Mr. Salami is our teacher. He is a good teacher. He is a weight lifter. He is also a mountain climber. He was a boxer, too, but he quit. Mr. Salami is 63 inches tall. He weighs 206 pounds.

Mr. Salami likes adventure stories. He reads to us on Mondays, Wednesdays, and Fridays. He reads stories about pirates and cowboys and explorers in the frozen North. All in all, Mr. Salami is very satisfactory.

Mr. Salami told us we were going to make turkeys out of paper. First, we would color the paper. Then, we would cut out the turkeys.

Mr. Salami was going to put our turkeys up on the walls. They were decorations for Thanksgiving.

Thanksgiving Potatoes

"Do you have turkey at your house?"
Big Gloria asked me.

"No, Gloria," I said. "We do not eat
turkey. We do not eat any kind of meat.
We are vegetarians."

"Vegetarians?"

"Yes. That means we do not eat meat. We only eat things that grow in the earth, and milk and cheese."

"I will be a vegetarian, too," Big Gloria said.

"You are right," I said. "Eating turkeys is wrong. We should not make them as decorations."

"Mr. Salami," Big Gloria said. "Bob and I will not make turkeys."

"Why not?" Mr. Salami asked. "Why won't you make turkeys?"

"Because we don't believe in it," Gloria said.

"You don't believe in turkeys?" Mr. Salami asked.

"We don't believe people should eat them," Big Gloria said. "We are vegetarians."

"So you will not draw a turkey, and you will not cut it out?" Mr. Salami asked.

"We will not," Big Gloria said.

"What will you draw? What will you cut out?" Mr. Salami asked.

"We will draw potatoes," I said. "We will draw potatoes and we will cut them out. We see nothing wrong with eating potatoes."

"Very well," Mr. Salami said. "Bob and Gloria and anyone else who wishes may make Thanksgiving potatoes."

Some other kids decided they would make potatoes, too.

Gloria and I drew excellent potatoes and cut them out carefully.

"Bob, are you really a vegetarian?" Gloria asked me.

"No," I said. "I just made that up."

"So, you fooled the teacher?" Gloria asked.

"Some people are vegetarians," I said. "I could be one. Are you really a vegetarian?"

"I never heard of a vegetarian until just now," Big Gloria said.

"So, you fooled the teacher," I said.

Gloria thought for a while. "I might become a vegetarian some day," Gloria said. "Poor turkeys."

Then she thought some more. "Good one, Bob," she said.

"I know," I said.

Everyone said our Thanksgiving potatoes were very good. Mr. Salami said so, too.

After School

After school, Big Gloria and I were walking home.

Billy Thimble and Tina Tiny caught up with us.

"Do not squash us," Tina Tiny said.

"Okay," Big Gloria said.

"We want to walk with you," Billy Thimble said to Big Gloria.

"Thank you," Big Gloria said.

"Okay," I said. We walked along.

"Your Thanksgiving potato was good," Billy Thimble said to Big Gloria.

"Thank you," Big Gloria said.

"Your potato was good also," Tina Tiny told me.

"Thank you," I said.

"We made Thanksgiving potatoes, too," Tina Tiny said.

"Mine was a killer potato from space," Billy Thimble said.

"I know," I said. "It was a cool potato."

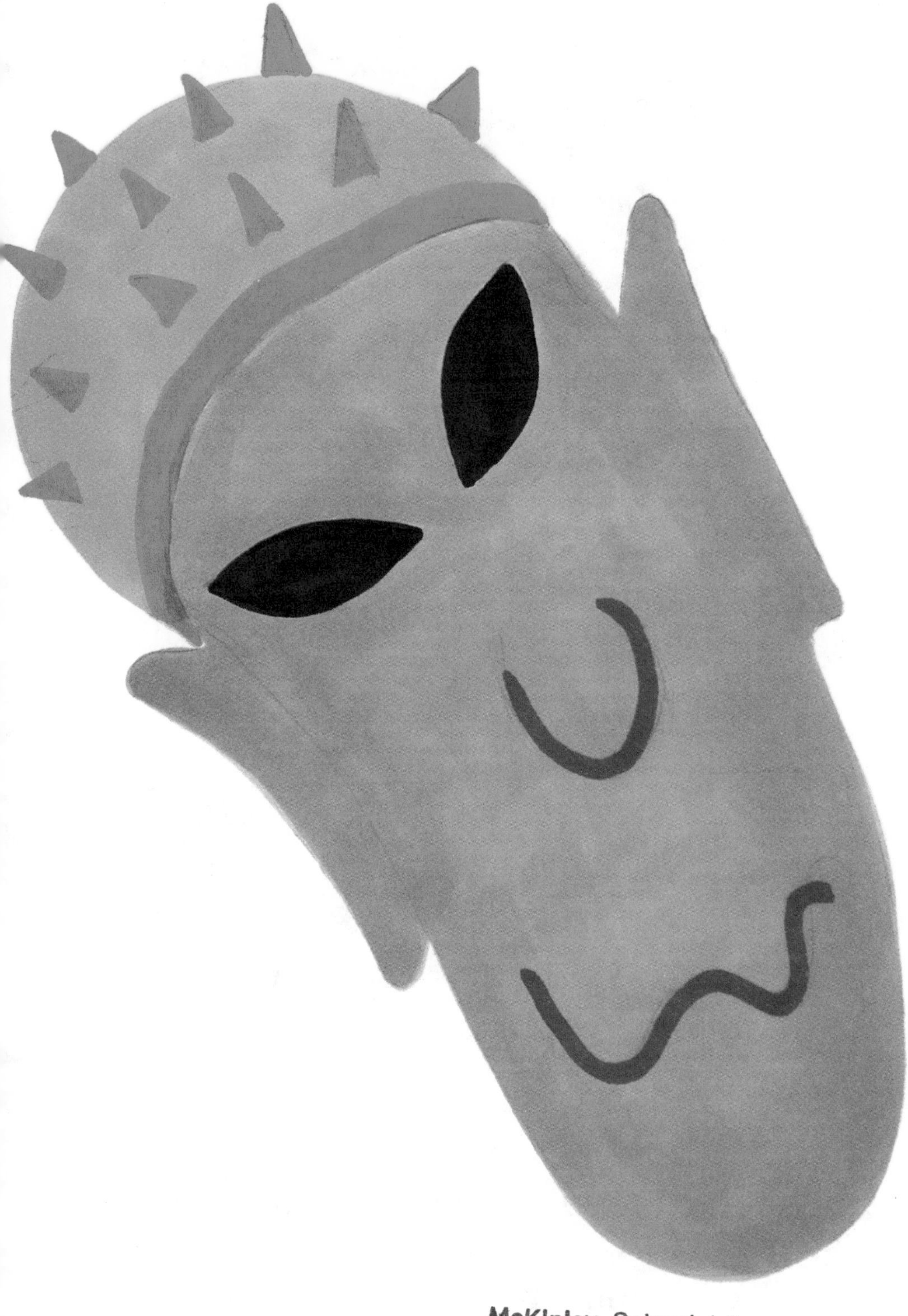

"Mine was a TV-star potato, with red lips," Tina Tiny said.

"I saw it," Big Gloria said. "It was good."

"Are you really vegetarians?" Billy Thimble asked.

"No," I said. "We just made that up."

"You fooled the teacher? You fooled Mr. Salami?" Tina Tiny asked.

"Yes," Big Gloria said.

"Do you think he really believed you?" Billy Thimble asked.

"He let us make Thanksgiving potatoes," I said.

"Tomorrow, we will tell him the truth," Gloria said.

"What do you think he will do?" Tina Tiny asked.

"I think he will laugh," I said.